Miners and Drillers

Tony Hyland

A+

Smart Apple Media

Smart Apple Media
2140 Howard Drive West
North Mankato
Minnesota 56003

First published in 2005 by
MACMILLAN EDUCATION AUSTRALIA PTY LTD
627 Chapel Street, South Yarra, Australia 3141

Visit our website at www.macmillan.com.au

Associated companies and representatives throughout the world.

Copyright © Tony Hyland 2005

Library of Congress Cataloging-in-Publication Data

Hyland, Tony.
    Miners and drillers / by Tony Hyland.
    p. cm. – (Extreme jobs)
    Includes index.
    ISBN-13: 978-1-58340-741-7
    1. Coal miners—Vocational guidance—Juvenile literature. 2. Well drillers—Vocational guidance—Juvenile literature. 3. Coal miners—Juvenile literature. 3. Well drillers—Juvenile literature. I. Title.

    HD8039.M6151195 2006
    622'.3023—dc22   2005056805

Edited by Ruth Jelley
Text and cover design by Peter Shaw
Page layout by SPG
Photo research by Legend Images
Illustration by Melissa Webb

Printed in USA

Acknowledgments
The author is grateful for the assistance provided by Xstrata Coal, ExxonMobil and Schlumberger Oilfield Services in arranging interviews for this book.
The author and the publisher are grateful to the following for permission to reproduce copyright material:

Cover photograph: At work on an ocean oil rig, courtesy of Jiri Lochman/Lochman Transparencies.

AAP/AP Photo, pp. 28 top, 29; Australian Picture Library/Corbis, pp. 10, 11, 14; Coo-ee Historical Picture Library, p. 13; Coo-ee Picture Library, p. 18; Esso Australia, p. 25 (both); Getty Images, pp. 8, 21, 23, 28 bottom; Sean Gallup/Getty Images, p. 6; Hulton Archive/Getty Images, p. 12; Jiri Lochman/Lochman Transparencies, pp. 1, 4, 20; Marie Lochman/Lochman Transparencies, p. 5; Dennis Sarson/Lochman Transparencies, pp. 17, 30; Alex Steffe/Lochman Transparencies, p. 7 top; France-Dominique Louie, pp. 26, 27 (both); Photolibrary. com, pp. 9, 16, 19, 24; Picture Media/Reuters, p. 22; Xstrata Coal, p. 15.

While every care has been taken to trace and acknowledge copyright, the publisher tenders their apologies for any accidental infringement where copyright has proved untraceable. Where the attempt has been unsuccessful, the publisher welcomes information that would redress the situation.

Contents

Glossary words
When a word is printed in **bold**, you can look up its meaning in the Glossary on page 31.

Do you want to be a miner or driller?

Drillers use large machinery in oil fields.

Our modern world depends on oil and electricity.

We use plastics and metals, such as steel and aluminum, every day. Have you ever wondered where they all come from?

Around the world, miners dig for coal and iron, and for precious metals such as gold and silver. Drillers operate oil wells on land, in swamps, and under the ocean floor. They provide fuel for our cars and raw material for our plastics.

Mining and drilling are extreme jobs. Whether it is under the ground or on an oil rig in the ocean, the work is sometimes hard and can be dangerous. But it is also an adventure.

Perhaps you could be a miner or driller one day.

Deep mining

Some coal mines are as deep as 9,800 feet (3,000 m) underground! The miners travel down to work in a huge elevator called a cage.

Wealth from underground

Our modern society could not work without the **minerals** and other resources that we dig from the earth, such as:

- coal, which is burned to make electricity

- iron **ore**, which is used to make steel

- **bauxite**, which is used to make aluminum

- copper, which is used for electrical wiring

- gold and silver, which are used in jewelry making

- stone, sand, and gravel which are used in construction

- salt, which is used for many different things, such as cooking and de-icing roads

- **petroleum**, which is used to make gas and oil for our cars, trucks, and other machines

- oil, which is used to make many plastics

- **natural gas**, which is used for heating and fuel

Mining and drilling produces many of the materials we need to run our modern transport system.

Life as a miner or driller

Life can be hard for miners. Miners work wherever the minerals are found. Few mines are close to cities. Most miners work in isolated places, such as deserts and mountains.

EXTREME INFO

A dangerous job

Although mining is safer now than it was in the past, it is still a dangerous job. Over 10,000 miners are killed every year around the world.

If an area has plenty of minerals, a town or city may develop nearby. The miners and their families live there. Mining towns are often far away from any other cities. Miners and their families sometimes feel isolated, so they usually form close-knit, friendly communities.

Mining can be dirty work. Digging coal and other minerals creates dust, which gets into the miners' clothes, hair, and skin. Coal dust can damage the miners' lungs.

Miners form close-knit communities and friendships.

Drilling for oil and gas

Oil and gas come from deep underground. Drilling teams drill holes down to the oil or gas **reservoir**. Then the oil

Oil rigs are isolated places.

and gas are pumped to the surface. Sometimes the oil is under strong pressure, and squirts to the surface as a **gusher**. Often the drill teams find that there is no oil in one spot. They seal up these **dry holes** and the team moves to another spot.

Oil companies sometimes drill for oil in swamps or under the sea. Huge **oil rigs** stand in the ocean, pumping oil from below the seabed. The oil is either collected by ships, or is piped directly to the shore. Oil rig workers live and work on the rig for days or even weeks, then take a long break on land.

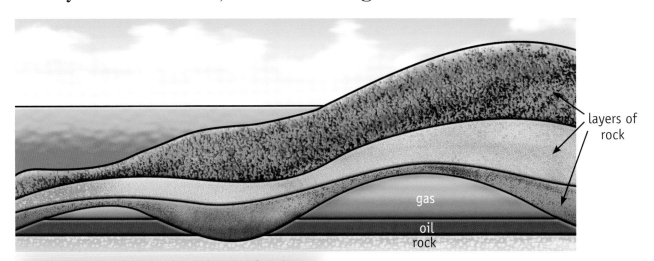

layers of rock

gas
oil
rock

Oil and gas collect between layers of rock.

Risks and dangers

Mining and drilling are risky jobs. There are many dangers, but experienced workers know what they are, and take care. Some of the risks are:

Cave-in	Underground mines sometimes collapse, trapping miners.
Poisonous gas	Miners sometimes uncover pockets of harmful gas, such as methane.
Accidents	Miners operate large, heavy machinery. Accidents can happen at any time.
Fire	Oil and natural gas burn easily. Drill workers cannot allow anything to happen that might set off a spark, which could start a fire.
Flood	Water sometimes seeps into mines from underground springs.
Explosions	Underground mines and oil wells can both explode.
Bad weather	Oil rig workers sometimes have to work in strong winds and high seas.
Lung disease	Coal dust causes a disease called black lung.
Noise	Mining and drilling machinery can be very noisy, and cause damage to people's hearing.

Working on an oil rig can be dangerous in bad weather.

Dealing with dust

Once, coal miners accepted that they had to breathe coal dust and could get black lung. Today, mining companies try to prevent dust. They spray the coal with water as it is mined. Some dust gets into the air, but huge fans quickly remove the dusty air. Modern **ventilation** equipment keeps fresh air pumping through the mines. Miners working in dusty conditions wear a **respirator**, which filters out the coal dust.

There can still be problems. Sometimes miners complain that the company is not doing enough to prevent dust being raised. Companies can be fined for allowing too much dust in a mine.

A miner wears a respirator to prevent breathing in any dust.

Training

There are several ways that miners and drillers can train to do their job. Some start as laborers, doing the hardest and dirtiest jobs. They learn their skills from experienced workers.

More often today, people who want to work in mining or oil drilling do a training course at a technical college. Here they learn mining and drilling techniques, and learn to handle machinery and explosives safely. Mining and drilling are dangerous jobs, so students learn safety procedures and first aid. Students can do part-time courses while working in mines or oil fields.

Many of the workers in mines and oil fields are skilled tradespeople such as electricians and mechanics. They keep the equipment in good order, and provide electricity for lighting and ventilation. Workers start in these trades as **apprentices**.

Mining apprentices learning their trade while they are working.

Advanced training

Workers in mines and drilling operations often go on to more advanced training. Large and complicated machinery is used in modern mines and oil fields.

These students are learning the techniques of modern mining.

Miners and drillers learn how to use this machinery. As new equipment is invented, they must learn how to use this, too.

The huge shovels and **draglines** used in **open cut** mines are sometimes controlled by computers. Experienced shovel operators have had to learn new computer skills in recent years.

Experienced miners and drillers usually learn to become the **foreman** of a work crew. The foreman must know how to use the equipment safely and how to lead a work team. Most countries have special training courses for foremen and other workers.

Some foremen go on to study **mine management** and become managers of the whole mine. They need to understand how each section of the mine works, and how to handle emergencies and accidents.

Digging into history

Early miners used picks and shovels to dig out coal.

Over 8,000 years ago, humans dug deep pits to get flint to make tools and weapons. The earliest copper and tin mines were dug over 5,000 years ago.

Mining has been around ever since humans learned to make metal tools and weapons. The ancient Romans mined iron for their weapons, gold and silver for jewelry, and stone for buildings.

In the 1800s, enormous amounts of coal were needed to run huge steam-powered factories. Coal miners worked in filthy, unsafe conditions using only picks and shovels. Thousands of miners died in accidents and many more died of black lung. Children as young as 10 years old worked underground for 12 or more hours a day.

Drilling in history

Drilling is a fairly new way of obtaining petroleum. For thousands of years, people knew about petroleum but had little use for it. It seeped out of the ground in some places. The ancient Egyptians coated their mummies with pitch, a sticky black substance made from petroleum.

In the 1850s, **kerosene** was discovered. It was made from petroleum and could be used for lighting lamps. Soon the first oil rush began, with hundreds of oil wells being drilled in the U.S. Shortly afterwards, other countries also began drilling for oil.

The invention of the internal combustion engine started the biggest demand for petroleum. By World War I (1914–18), petroleum fuels were used to power cars, trucks, ships, and airplanes.

Motor cars created a new demand for petroleum.

EXTREME INFO

Middle East oil

In the 1920s, huge deposits of petroleum were discovered in Iraq. Many countries in the Middle East now rely on money from sales of oil.

Mining and drilling jobs

Underground coal miners

EXTREME INFO

Coal dust explosion

Coal dust sometimes explodes violently. The largest mining disaster occurred in 1942 in China, when 1,549 miners were killed in a coal dust explosion.

Underground coal miners no longer use picks and shovels. Miners operate huge machines which rip out thousands of pounds of coal.

Coal miners operate a machine called a long-wall cutter. This huge circular cutter spins along a wall of coal, cutting a long section from the coal **seam**. The coal falls onto a conveyor belt, which takes it out of the mine. Huge steel roof supports hold the roof up behind the cutter. When the cutter finishes cutting a section, the cutter and the roof supports move forward automatically. The cutter then begins cutting a new section.

The miners often work several miles underground. Huge air conditioners suck out the moist, dirty air and pump in fresh air. Underground mines can be noisy as well as dirty. Miners often wear ear protectors.

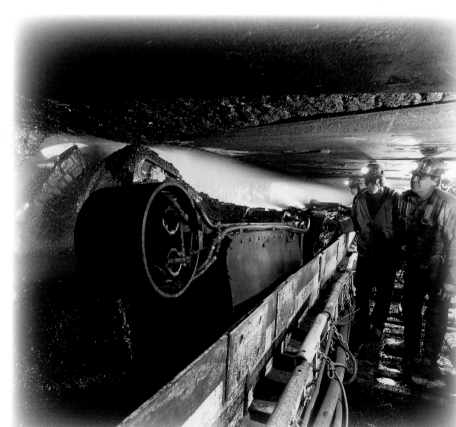

Miners operate a long-wall cutting machine.

14

PROFILE

Glen Lewis

Underground coal mine general manager

Glen Lewis works in an underground coal mine.

Job

I manage a group of five coal mines in New South Wales, Australia.

Experience

I did an **apprenticeship** as a mine electrician. I also studied to become a mine crew manager, then mine manager.

My work

I come from an old Welsh coal mining family. My Dad and Grandad were both coal miners.

My background

I regularly go underground with the mine managers to overview the operations. I watch, make comments if necessary, and talk to the miners.

Underground working conditions

It's **humid** and fairly dirty, but far better than it used to be. A lot of technology, time, and effort have gone into improving dust and roof control standards.

Safety underground

In my early days I saw some big cave-ins, where we had to run to stay alive. Technology has greatly improved the way we do our job.

Mining and drilling jobs

Open cut miners

When the minerals are not far below the surface, miners dig an open cut mine. They scoop the minerals from a large hole in the ground. Stone is often cut from an open cut mine called a quarry.

Coal, iron ore, and bauxite are usually mined in open cut mines. Explosives experts blow up whole sections of the mine wall, bringing down tons of material. Miners operating huge power shovels and earth-moving equipment scoop up the minerals. The ore is loaded onto conveyor belts or huge trucks and taken to the processing plant.

EXTREME INFO

World's largest robot

The world's largest robot is actually a coal shovel called a dragline. It weighs 3,400 tons (3.5 million kg). The operators control the machine with computers, rather than levers.

These large machines move tons of material.

Mine truck drivers

Mine truck drivers operate the world's largest trucks in open cut mines. Drivers use these huge trucks to haul enormous loads of ore from the mine to the processing plant. The truck drivers climb a ladder to reach the cabin. Once inside, they must drive slowly and carefully. The trucks are not easy to control, and turning corners is difficult. Mine trucks are far too big to travel on normal highways. They are only used on the mine site.

Mine truck drivers need a truck license before they can drive these huge machines. They learn to control the trucks at the mine site.

The wheels on this truck are taller than the driver.

RISK FACTOR

Open cut miners lead a hard life outdoors. There are risks in their work, such as:

- explosives accidents
- machinery accidents
- dirty conditions
- working in bad weather

Mining and drilling jobs

Opal miners

Opal miners search for opal, a sparkling gemstone that is found in layers of rock under the ground. They do not use large machinery. Opal can be easily crushed or broken, so most opal miners dig by hand.

Opal miners dig a deep hole called a shaft down through the dirt to the opal seam. Miners may use bulldozers or explosives to clear away the overburden, the layer of dirt above the seam.

Once they find the seam, opal miners chip away carefully with a small pick. Often they find nothing but potch, colorless opal with no value. Good quality opals have bright flashes of red and blue shining through them.

An opal miner uses hand tools rather than machinery.

Living in opal country

Opal miners live in small, isolated towns, such as Coober Pedy and Lightning Ridge in Australia. Most of the world's opal comes from mines in the hot Australian desert. Opal miners in these desert towns have found an unusual way to live in the fierce desert heat. Many of their homes are underground. The miners and their families live in old mines or in holes that they have dug specially for homes. Underground homes are cool and comfortable. They are not dusty or smelly, and can be kept quite clean.

Above ground there is little to see except for piles of dirt from old mines and a few buildings. Even shops and churches are underground.

RISK FACTOR

Opal miners work in small, narrow tunnels underground. They face risks, such as:

- equipment accidents
- explosions
- cave-ins
- lack of fresh air

Buildings are built underground in desert mining towns.

Mining geologists and engineers

Mining geologists and engineers research and plan mining operations. They do some of their work on computers, but they also do hands-on work.

Mining geologists are experts on rocks and minerals. They are college-trained scientists. Their job is to work out exactly what minerals are under the ground and where they are.

Geologists often spend time camped out in rugged country. They may work with a small survey team, trying to locate mineral deposits in unexplored territory. Sometimes geologists do mining surveys from the air. They fly in small airplanes or helicopters low over the ground. Their electronic equipment can detect and measure the minerals in the ground below.

A geologist surveys mineral deposits before mining begins.

EXTREME INFO

Fossil hunters

Geologists studying rocks sometimes find fossils of prehistoric plants or animals. They can tell how old the fossils are by working out the age of the rocks they were found in.

Mining engineers

Mining engineers plan mines and work out the best way to get the coal or minerals from the ground. Mining engineers learn their skills at college. They must know the different types of machinery used in mining. They are responsible for the safety of the mine. They check the walls and roofs to see that they are strong, and make sure that clean air can get to the miners. Engineers sometimes design new types of machinery, such as cutting machines and automatic roof supports.

Mining engineers often work for international companies. They may travel or work overseas, learning how mines are built in other countries.

Engineering and geology students often work in mines during their vacation time, to gain useful experience.

RISK FACTOR

Engineers and geologists work in difficult conditions. They face risks in their work such as:

- equipment accidents
- explosions
- mine collapses

Mining engineers plan the mining process.

Oil drilling crews

Oil drilling crews operate drills that bore down to petroleum, which is buried deep underground.

Oil drilling crews first erect the derrick. This is the tall framework that will hold the drilling equipment. An engine room beside the derrick provides power for turning the drill. The **drill bit** has a set of rotating steel teeth tipped with diamond or **tungsten**, two of the hardest materials known. As the drill bit bores into the earth, the crew adds more sections of pipe so that it can go deeper. When the drill bit becomes worn, the crew raises the whole pipe, removing each section as it comes up. A new drill bit is attached, and the equipment is lowered down the drill-hole again.

An oil worker inspects the drilling machinery.

Drilling workers

Oil drilling crews are always busy, adding sections of pipe and keeping their equipment in good working order. Their work often takes them far away from comfortable city life.

Drill crew workers have names that seem to match their tough jobs. Roustabouts are the laborers on the crew. They handle the heavy pipes and clean the work area. Roughnecks are in charge of the laboring crew. Drillers operate the brake and motor of the drill, and decide how fast and deep the drill needs to go. Drillers make sure the workers follow strict safety rules, as the work can be dangerous. Tool pushers control the whole drilling operation. They plan the work schedule, making sure that the oil well is completed on time.

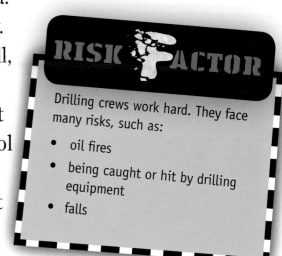

RISK FACTOR

Drilling crews work hard. They face many risks, such as:

- oil fires
- being caught or hit by drilling equipment
- falls

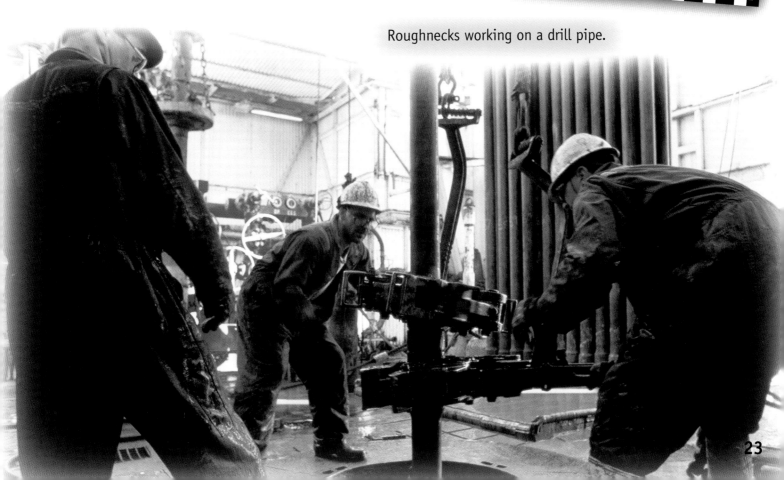

Roughnecks working on a drill pipe.

23

Mining and drilling jobs

Offshore oil rig workers

Offshore oil rig workers work on large oil rigs at sea. Much of the world's oil lies offshore, deep under the seabed. The oil rigs are used to drill for this oil, then pump it to shore.

In water up to 525 feet (160 m) deep, oil rigs stand on the seabed. In deep ocean areas, huge floating platforms are anchored to the seabed.

Oil rigs are like small towns in the middle of the ocean. Workers live there for a week or more. Cooks prepare all the meals, and cleaners keep the rooms clean. The workers work long, hard shifts. In their leisure time they can watch television, read, or surf the Internet. After working on the rig for a few weeks, the workers take a few weeks off. They fly back to land by helicopter.

An oil rig worker using machinery on an offshore oil rig.

EXTREME INFO

Danger at sea

An oil rig is a dangerous place to be during an explosion or a fierce storm. It can be difficult to rescue the crew from an isolated oil rig in these conditions.

PROFILE

Bill Wilson

Bill Wilson supervises an offshore oil pumping platform.

Offshore platform supervisor

Job

I manage the Kingfish B oil platform in Bass Strait, Australia.

My work

We pump oil from 1.6 miles (2.5 km) under the seabed. We work seven days on the rig then have seven days off.

My staff

This place is busy. We have maintenance workers, mechanics, electricians, and radio operators. We also have a chef and catering staff. Other work crews, such as divers and painters, come through sometimes.

Bass Strait weather

The weather can quickly become severe in Bass Strait. We get winds up to 60 miles (100 km) an hour and waves 50 to 65 feet (15-20 m) high. Oil platforms are designed to stand up to any weather the ocean can throw at us.

My favorite time

My favorite time is the end of the day, when I can watch a magnificent sunset and see dolphins swimming past the rig.

Off the platform

Like many of the workers here, my life on shore is completely separate. I have a farm where I raise highland cattle.

Bill Wilson wears safety gear at work on the oil platform.

Offshore oil engineers

Specially trained engineers supervise offshore oil rigs. They lower electronic measuring tools down the well to check what is at the bottom of the oil well.

Wireline field engineers control this measuring equipment. They travel from rig to rig, setting up their equipment and recording data before moving on. Their wireline tools fit into long, narrow cylinders which are lowered down the well on a long chain. The tools are made in sections so that they can be fitted together and lowered into the well. The data they gather is sent back along a cable and stored in a computer.

A complete set of tools can weigh around 1,100 pounds (500 kg), and be lowered 9,800 feet (3,000 m) below the seabed. A powerful winch is used to lower the tools into the well.

EXTREME INFO

No shutdowns

Offshore oil platforms operate all day, every day. Workers do 12-hour shifts. Even on holidays such as Christmas, someone has to keep working.

Oil field engineers transport all of their equipment in a truck.

PROFILE

France-Dominique Louie

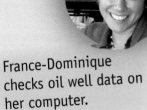

Oilfield engineer

Job

I work as a wireline field engineer on oil rigs in the Gulf of Mexico.

France-Dominique checks oil well data on her computer.

My most exciting experience

Working in the jungle in Venezuela, where jobs last five days nonstop and I had to run very complicated tools. At night I slept in a hammock between my truck and a tree.

My job can be dangerous

It is often hard physical work. We carry heavy equipment. We also deal with radioactive sources and explosives.

Bad weather

In bad weather I have to put my slicker suit on and confront the wind, rain, or whatever! It can very easily become muddy and hectic, but the job has to continue. A rig never shuts down, so the workers have to keep working. Of course, in extreme weather conditions such as hurricanes, everything comes to a halt.

France-Dominique Louie at work on an oil platform in the Gulf of Mexico.

Mining and drilling jobs

Firefighters battle an oil field blaze.

Oil well firefighters

Oil well fires are fierce and dangerous. Firefighters need special skills to put them out.

Oil wells are always at risk of fire. Oil workers take careful precautions against fires. If an oil well does catch fire, it is difficult to put out. The fire can burn for months, feeding off oil from deep in the well. Modern oil wells have a **cut-off valve**, which shuts off this supply of fuel.

Teams of highly trained firefighters fly in from around the world to fight oil well fires. Oil well firefighters have developed unusual methods for putting out fires. One method is to set off an explosion at the well-head. This can blast the flame out, just as you can blow out a match. Firefighters also try to cover the well-head with mud or large concrete blocks.

Paul "Red" Adair

The most famous oil well firefighter was Paul "Red" Adair. He led a team of firefighters who battled the worst oil well fires. His team fought over 2,000 fires all over the world. Adair died in 2004, but his methods are still used to fight oil well fires.

Adair was the first to use many of today's oil well firefighting tactics. His teams put out fires that ordinary firefighters could not get near. One fire that he put out in the Sahara desert burned with flames 650 feet (200 m) high.

In 1991, Red Adair's team fought the fires in the oil fields of Kuwait. Over 700 oil well fires had been deliberately lit by the retreating Iraqi army. Despite the dangers, none of Adair's team ever suffered a serious injury.

Red Adair traveled out to the Piper Alpha oil rig to fight the fire there in 1988.

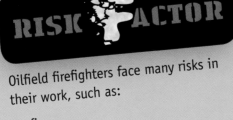

RISK FACTOR

Oilfield firefighters face many risks in their work, such as:

- fire
- explosions
- accidents with firefighting equipment

Could you be a miner or driller?

You could be a miner or driller if you:

- have normal health

- are fit and energetic

- enjoy being active outdoors

- are responsible and hardworking

- are not afraid of tight spaces

If you become a tradesperson, such as a mechanic or an electrician, your skills could get you an interesting job in mining or drilling. If you prefer to be an engineer or a scientist, you could study engineering or geology at college. You'll spend a lot of time out in the field.

Is there a mining museum near your home? If so, spend a few hours there. You might find that mining is the life for you.

Mining or drilling could be just the right job for you.

Glossary

apprentices	people who learn a trade while working at it
apprenticeship	the period of being an apprentice; generally four years
bauxite	ore that aluminum is made from
cut-off valve	a device for cutting off the flow of oil
draglines	large mining shovels which are dragged along the ground
drill bit	the cutting end of a mining drill
dry holes	drill holes that produce no oil
foreman	the boss of a small group of workers
gusher	oil well from which oil pours out under pressure
humid	when there is a lot of moisture in the air
kerosene	fuel oil made from petroleum
mine management	control of an entire mining operation
minerals	substances that are mined from the ground
natural gas	gas that is found underground
oil rigs	large platforms holding oil-drilling crews and equipment
open cut	method of mining by removing the top surface from a layer of minerals
ore	rock from which metals are extracted
petroleum	oil as it occurs naturally underground
quartz	a very hard crystal rock
reservoir	large natural pool of liquid or gas
respirator	a device which is worn over the face to prevent gas or dust being inhaled
seam	a layer of mineral such as coal or opal
tungsten	extremely hard metal
ventilation	air conditioning system which takes out dirty air and pumps in fresh air

Index